W9-CCN-362

MONSTER MADNESS!

By Billy Wrecks
Illustrated by Erik Doescher, Mike DeCarlo, and David Tanguay

A Random House PICTUREBACK® Book
Random House New York

DC SUPER FRIENDS and all related titles, characters, and elements are trademarks of DC Comics. Copyright © 2011 DC Comics. All rights reserved. Published in the United States by Random House Children's Books, a division of Random House, Inc., 1745 Broadway, New York, NY 10019, and in Canada by Random House of Canada Limited, Toronto. Pictureback, Random House, and the Random House colophon are registered trademarks of Random House, Inc.
www.randomhouse.com/kids
Library of Congress Control Number: 2010927311
ISBN: 978-0-375-87230-3
Printed in the United States of America
10 9 8 7 6 5 4 3

The city of Metropolis threw a big costume party on Halloween night to thank the Super Friends for all the times they had saved the city. The Super Friends came dressed as themselves! Everyone was having fun.

But someone sinister was lurking in the shadows—someone who wasn't happy. It was . . .

. . . Scarecrow!

"The Super Friends have ruined my plans too many times," the creepy criminal growled. "Let's see how they like it when I ruin their party!"

Scarecrow leaped into the middle of the crowd. Everyone screamed as a foul-smelling fog poured out of Scarecrow's jack-o'-lantern and filled the room.

"My latest mind-bending gas will make these partygoers think they *are* what they're dressed as!" Scarecrow cried. "The Super Friends will be fighting a roomful of monsters!"

"Get them!" Scarecrow snarled. The costumed people attacked the Super Friends. The werewolf howled! The zombie lurched! The vampire bared his fangs! The pirates brandished their swords! And the witch cackled!

"Be careful!" Batman warned the Super Friends. "We don't want to hurt them. We just want to slow them down until we can find a way to stop Scarecrow!"

The vampire hissed as he tried to bite Batman's neck, but Batman was too fast for him.

"Try the punch bowl if you're *that* thirsty," Batman said. He used his Batrope to lasso the vampire.

Across the room, the werewolf was chasing Green Lantern.
"I know just what to do with a bad dog like you," Green
Lantern said, scooping the growling werewolf into a giant green
dogcatcher's net made with his power ring.

The zombie was slow but strong. Superman didn't want to hurt the monstrous party guest, but the zombie kept coming!

"It's time to get this ghoul tucked in for the night," Superman said, using his heat vision to cut some ghost decorations loose. The ghosts fluttered down from the ceiling, and the zombie became hopelessly entangled in the sheets and ropes.

Cyborg and Aquaman were busy with their own fight. The pirates and the witch might just have been party guests, but their swords and broom were real enough. *Ouch!*

Meanwhile, a black cat was chasing Robin—and her claws were razor sharp!
"I know that cats love to chase birds," Robin said as he dodged the claws
again and again. "But I think this kitty wants *me* for a snack!"
"Snacks!" Batman exclaimed. "That's it!"

"Not all the guests at this party are monsters," Batman
said. "And I know just the pair of partiers to give Scarecrow
a taste of his own bad medicine!"

Batman grabbed a big bowl of popcorn and dumped it on
Scarecrow's head! Two human-sized crows took notice. *Yum!*

"What do you think you're doing, Bat-brain?" Scarecrow yelled.
Then he realized that there was popcorn stuck in every nook and
cranny of his costume—and those crows looked hungry! "UH-OH!"

Scarecrow ran off into the night, chased by the giant crows.
"Those birds will keep Scarecrow busy for a while," Batman said.
"And as for everyone else, they'll be safe and sound right here.
The effects of Scarecrow's gas should wear off by midnight."
"Until then," the Super Friends said together, "let's . . .